To Von Ryan's Express ~ KG
For Codie & Kyle ~ GP

Bloomsbury Publishing, London, Oxford, New York, New Delhi and Sydney

First published in Great Britain in 2016 by Bloomsbury Publishing Plc
50 Bedford Square, London, WC1B 3DP

www.bloomsbury.com

BLOOMSBURY is a registered trademark of Bloomsbury Publishing Plc

Text copyright © Kes Gray 2016
Illustrations copyright © Garry Parsons 2016
The moral rights of the author and illustrator have been asserted

A CIP catalogue record of this book is available from the British Library

ISBN 978 1 4088 6598 9 (HB)
ISBN 978 1 4088 6599 6 (PB)
ISBN 978 1 4088 6600 9 (eBook)

All papers used by Bloomsbury Publishing are natural, recyclable products made
from wood grown in well managed forests. The manufacturing processes
conform to the environmental regulations of the country of origin

Printed in China by Leo Paper Products, Heshan, Guangdong

1 3 5 7 9 10 8 6 4 2

# Nuddy Ned's
# Christmas

Kes Gray
and
Garry Parsons

BLOOMSBURY
LONDON OXFORD NEW YORK NEW DELHI SYDNEY

Fairy lights a-twinkling,
Stockings neatly hung.
Turkey stuffed and parsnips peeled –
The Christmas prep was done.

Stretched out on the sofa,
Munching hot mince pies,
Ned's mum and dad sighed happily,
Then closed their weary eyes.

Full of wild excitement –
Supposed to be asleep –
Nuddy Ned sat up in bed
And gave up counting sheep.

Tearing off his jim-jams
He hurtled down the stairs,
Catching both his mum and dad
Completely unawares.

His mum's face froze with horror.
His dad's eyes opened wide.
But before they could say, 'Mistletoe',
Ned had run outside!

"Nuddy Ned, Nuddy Ned,
Where do you think you're going?
It's Christmas Eve! It's minus three!
And can't you see it's snowing?!"

Ned danced round the garden
Like a proper silly billy.
Snowflakes swirling around his head
(And places like his . . . belly button).

"Yahoo!" said Ned. "Wahey!" said Ned,
Heading for the street.

"It's Christmas Eve!
It's Christmas Eve!
There's someone I **must** meet!"

Santa's sleigh was on its way,
Just leaving Lanzarote.
"Goodness gracious!" Blitzen cried.
"Did I just see a botty?"

The reindeers peered down through the clouds.
"I saw it too!" said Cupid.
Santa frowned and flicked the reins,
"A botty? Don't be stupid!"

Mum and Dad jumped in the car,
"We're going to catch you, Ned!"
Dad turned the key then thumped the wheel.
The battery was dead.

"Ned, come back, you naughty boy,
The temperatures are freezing!"
"Not for me!" laughed Nuddy Ned.
"I find them rather pleasing!"

Ned sped through the icy streets,
Turning snow to slush.
"What fun!" said Ned.
"How cool," laughed Ned.
"I've made a snowman blush!"

Ned galloped through the precinct –
Minus his apparel.

He skidded past the library
Then heard a Christmas carol.

Carol singers all wrapped up
In duffle coats and parkas,
Dropped their song sheets,
Turned and screamed,
"NED'S COMPLETELY STARKERS!"

Ned ran to the town hall
Then, rather cheekily,
Jumped up like a monkey
And climbed the Christmas tree.

The tree, shipped in from Lapland,
Was thirty metres high.
Ned climbed to the very top
And waved at the night sky.

"Santa, are you up there?
Can you see me down below?
I know that you are busy,
But I'd love to say hello."

The sound of sleigh bells filled the air.
The sky began to twinkle.
Ned removed the star on top
and covered up his winkle.

"Yahoo!" cried Ned.

"Wahey!" said Ned.

"I can't believe you're there!"

For Santa and his reindeers
Had landed in the square.

"Goodness me, Ned!" Santa squeaked.
"Haven't you been told?
You can't spend Christmas in the nude!
You'll catch your death of cold!"

Santa rummaged through his sacks
And pulled out some new clothes.
"I'll have you dressed in no time, Ned.
Here, try on some of those."

Ned smiled at all the jumpers,
Trousers, shirts and socks.
"No thanks, Santa," he replied.
"Being naked rocks!"

"I'm Nuddy Ned, I'm Nuddy Ned!
Autumn, winter, spring.
Running round with nothing on
is totally my thing!"

Santa stroked his snowy beard,
His chestnut eyes burned bright.
"Happy Christmas, Nuddy Ned . . .

I do believe
you're right!"